D1407652

ABOUT THE AUTHOR

Check Ty The Hunter's website to
see a complete list of books.

"The World Keepers" -
Tween/Teen readers

"The Guild Crafters" -
Tween/Teen Readers

"The Guild Crafters Block Books"
- New Readers

COME FIND TY ON YOUTUBE @ TY THE HUNTER

Get in touch with me at
theworldkeepersbooks@gmail.com

Chapter 1

Thomas, here.

You know who I am, right? I mean, I know Jed talks A LOT about himself, but he must have mentioned me, the excellent older brother?

Ringing any bells?

Here, let me remind you of the role he "says" I've played in this little fiasco so far.

I'm the surly older brother who used to be fun but now sucks. I don't talk to him, I never play with him, and when he asks me questions, I look at him like he's annoying.

He got pulled into Roblox, and I wasn't there to help him, but Kat was. (Pay attention to that, because it's going to get real critical, real fast).

Jed took it upon himself to snoop, even though he says he's not that guy, and ended up in the game again.

THEN, oh yes, there's more, THEN he lost my dog in there as well!

And finally, I get home to find him hopping mad, accusing me of all sorts of nefarious plans, demanding answers and threatening to tell my parents if I don't give him those answers.

Now you have Jed's side of things.

You know what they say about stories?

There are three sides to each.

His side.

My side.

And, the truth.

It's time you heard the truth.

Alright, let's get down to brass tacks. We've just established that I know what you've been up to, I know who you've been talking to, and I know you're thinking Jed must be some kind of hero.

"Ooooh" (this is you I'm mimicking, by the way), "What a good brother he is, how awful for Thomas to give him the cold shoulder. I can't believe he'd send Jed back into that game, he's just a BABY!"

Were you thinking that? Of course, you were!

None of that stuff actually happened though.

Sure, Jed did go into Roblox, sure he lost my dog, sure he's in it up to his ears at this point, but none of that stuff had a thing to do with me.

I'll explain more as we go on, but there are a few things you need to know right now.

First, I never wanted Jed involved in any of this, I don't even want to be involved in it.

Second, the message Jed got about the zombie game? Remember that? It didn't come from me. Don't believe me? Check with my mom. I bet she'll tell you that particular part of the conversation came in as a text after she got off the phone with my dad.

Third, there is one person in all of this who needs us to cooperate. One person who (I think) has way more going on than we've been told.

Now that we're all on the same page, kind of, I'm going to start at the beginning.

When I'm done, and only when I'm done, will you be allowed to sit back, relax, and draw your own conclusions.

I was Jumping way before Jed even knew what Jumping was, and there's a whole lot more to it than he knows.

There's probably a whole lot more to it than I know.

All that matters in this situation is that I know more than him, and I know she planned for him to get involved all along.

"She, who," you ask?

Kat, of course.

Oh, are you shocked? Were you thinking she was some sort of innocent bystander?

More like the ringleader.

I don't have any solid information to back this up, yet, but I know that she's the one who got me involved, she's the one who got Jed involved, and I wouldn't be surprised to know that she got Jake involved.

For sure she's the one who brought Jed into Roblox. I mean "in to" like he was there, not just that she told him about it.

Did she know he Jumped like that? Maybe not.

Maybe so.

Did I confuse you again? Are you like "Jumped like what?"

Jumped like INTO Roblox!

I can't do that, not even close. I don't know if Kat can do it, I also don't know if Jake or Dirk can do it.

Somehow, I doubt they can, because from the moment Kat found out I had a younger brother, she's been asking me about him, dropping hints (some subtle, some not so subtle) about seeing if he could Jump as well.

I always refused, and she never really pressed.

The moment I go out of town without him though, what happens?

He "accidentally" ends up in the game.

Oh sure, Jed told me all about how he thought it was her fault, and how she said that it wasn't supposed to be him that came through.

But I KNOW it wasn't supposed to be me that came through because Kat already KNEW that I couldn't use the portals.

She's known that for months!

Uh huh, I see your brain working now. Coming around to the idea that all may not be as it seems, are we?

Good.

I'll get back to that later, or rather I'll get back to it by telling you a different part of the story

I've been playing the Roblox for years, I'm a "veteran" which means you have a certain amount of time under your belt, I've built my own games, created my own worlds, and met all sorts of people.

It really is the perfect game.

Too perfect, as I'm coming to see.

Anyhow, here I am, on the way home from hunting for a week with my dad. You've heard all about that as well, I presume.

Post isn't that small of a city, despite what Jed says. The population is more like 5,000, and that's not counting cows.

The rest of what he said is probably correct.

It's a long 8 hours up there, and a long 8 hours back. I have no cell phone because I left it at home, so I figured I'd take the time to give you my side of things.

I was thinking about where to start with all of this, but now that I've mentioned Kat, I think I'll start with her.

That seems like as good a place as any.

I met Kat in a game called "Soro's Restaurant".

I know you're wondering why anyone would want to play a game that has you work in a restaurant, but hey, I'm 12. I'm barely allowed to use the microwave in real life, so pretending to cook over flaming ovens is awesome!

It's not for real money, of course, but at the time, I thought there was a bit of prestige that went along with getting that job. It's not like you just walk in and work there, it's actually a whole process.

Getting the job was half the fun. More than half the fun, really.

Have you ever heard the term "the thrill of the chase"?

That's what it was.

I did enjoy working there, for a while at least.

Or at least, I thought I was enjoying it.

More on that, later.

Soro's was this place where I'd go to hang out. It was almost like a game about being social, you know? You'd go to the door, someone would seat you, someone else would take your order and deliver your food, etc.

Once I realized you actually had to apply to get those positions, I wanted to get a job there. The idea consumed me, it was like the MOST important thing to me in the whole world, for a few weeks of my life.

To get the job, I had to interview online with a manager.

Sound simple, right?

Wrong.

First, you have to subscribe to the game feed so that you know when the interviews are going to take place. They give you a link so you can join a chatroom, and the chat room opens up a few minutes before the interview begins.

Once you join, you just have to hope you get a good interviewer, someone who isn't on a total power trip.

That's a thing, you know? People on the internet getting all crazy when they have a little control.

Especially kids!

Not hating on my age group or anything, but we have so little control at this point in our lives that when we get it....watch out!

I had to interview three times before I got hired.

#jerks

Turns out, they don't really want you if you aren't capable of typing and using proper grammar.

All those times mom lectured me about learning to type, paying attention to punctuation and pronouns.

She was right.

Who knew?

Really, life hack here, lay off the lazy texting stuff right now, forever, you'll thank me later.

Spelling is your friend.

Back to the story.

If you do get hired, you start working. There are quite a few jobs to do, but you can't do all of them right off the bat.

You have to work your way up in the ranks, but I never did, so I got to choose between being a host (seating people) or being a waiter.

I chose waiter.

If you work long enough, you might get a promotion. If you don't work often enough, you get demoted and lose your job, etc.

I'm not sure why this felt like such a huge moment, getting that job at Soro's, it's not like you get any money from it, but still, it felt like I was doing something important.

That should have been my first clue.

Anyhow, off topic there.

This is what I was getting around to with all of that information. I had to interview to work at Soro's, and guess who interviewed me?

Did you get it in one?

If you guessed "Kat", you did!

Kat interviewed me, I'm fantastic, she hired me, and we became friends in the game.

I thought she hired me because I'm awesome, but now, knowing what I know, I wonder if it wasn't just the opening she was looking for.

After we'd been friends and worked together for a while, Kat started talking to me in chat. Just a bit at first, probably so I wouldn't think she was a creeper, but then more often. Until it got the point that we'd talk every single day.

The conversations got longer, we got to know each other better. You know how that stuff goes.

One day I ended up telling her about these dreams I'd always have. Not like uncomfortable/weird dreams, just regular weird. And since they were always about Roblox, it made perfect sense to share.

The dreams were always pretty much the same:

I'd wake up from a deep sleep and lay there for a minute trying to figure out what woke me. Turning my head on my pillow, I'd notice the light from my computer screen. It illuminates the entire room, and I know that if I don't shut the laptop, I'll never get back to sleep.

So I get up out of bed, walk over to my computer desk, and reach down to close the lid.

Before I do it, I glance at the screen and see that I have Roblox pulled up, only it's not a world I've ever played in before.

I've got a bird's eye view of a small city. There are buildings, streets, a park, a school. It looks like an ordinary town in the middle of anywhere.

My view shifts and I find myself looking specifically at the park. Several characters are playing. Some are riding bikes, a group is playing basketball, and one is kicking around on a little scooter while wearing a snake around his neck.

The scooter rider notices me, which is odd because I'm not in the game and all. But he sees me, it's obvious.

He rides to the middle of my screen, raises a hand, and waves.

I wave back.

He smiles and gestures with his hand, kind of a "come here" gesture.

I don't "come here" because it's a computer and this is a dream, but I do lean in closer.

This time, he says something. I don't know what he's saying, I can't really hear the words if that makes sense, but I can hear the tinny buzz of noise, and I know he's speaking to me.

"Come here", he repeats the gesture.

Only this time, in addition to the gesture, he holds his hand out, showing me something in it.

I can't see what it is, but it doesn't matter. In my dream, I NEED whatever it is he has in his hand.

So I reach for it.

I reach my hand all the way into the screen and into the game, intending to take the object he's offering.

Only, when I pull my hand out, instead of retrieving an object, I've retrieved him.

I bet Freud would have a field day with that!

It doesn't sound too odd, right? I mean it's just a dream, people have weird dreams all the time.

But this is where it gets really weird.

One day, after having this dream about 20 times, I woke up and noticed that there was a little action figure by my bed. An action figure that looks just like the little guy in my dream.

I didn't have any action figures like that. I don't even know if they make action figures like that.

I knew, at that moment, without a doubt, that I had grabbed that character and taken him out of Roblox.

I never told anyone about this until I told Kat.

When I did tell her, it was sort of like a "ha ha ha, you're really going to think I'm weird when I say this, but..."

She believed me though, and more than that, she became a lot more interested in me.

I didn't know why at the time, I figured she just thought my dream was funny, that I was a funny guy, and that she liked chatting with me.

Until the day she asked me to Jump.

Chapter 2

The day Kat asked me to Jump, I almost stopped talking to her altogether.

Even now I wonder if I should have followed that gut reaction.

I wonder if it would have saved me a lot of trouble.

I don't want you to get the wrong idea. She is responsible for some of this, for sure, but for a lot of it, for the root of it, she's just another pawn in a much larger game.

So while I wish she had at least left Jed out of it for a whole lot longer, I know that eventually, we'd all have taken our places on the game board.

When she sent me a message asking me to meet her at Soro's, I didn't think anything of it.

We'd often log in together, playing at working. She would host, and I'd take orders and serve. We'd send in-game "tells" to one another making fun of eccentric customers or complaining when we'd get someone who just could not be satisfied, despite our best efforts.

I would have said we were friends at that point, though it took me awhile to get there.

I was pretty sure she was harmless, but my mother had talked to me often enough about cyber creepers that I had to consider at least that Kat might be....what's the word I'm looking for......oh yes, completely crazy.

"Thomas," my mom would say, "you don't know who's on the other end of that internet connection. It could be a 60-year-old man who lives at home in his mother's basement and enjoys role-playing as a teenage girl."

"Mom, that doesn't really happen, does it?" I was horrified! I mean there's just no way, right?

"You bet it does, so watch yourself, I mean it. No personal information, none at all. If I catch wind of you doing anything like that, you'll be banned from electronics until you move out."

I didn't doubt she'd follow through on that threat, either.

She could get really worked up over this particular topic, so I learned to nod and agree.

More importantly, I learned to take it seriously.

I've been cyber-bullied a few times. Nothing too crazy, but enough to make me realize that people are entirely okay with hurting you if they can do it in the cloak of anonymity.

She tells me this wasn't a thing when she was growing up. "Thomas, we didn't have internet until I was almost 20 years old. I got my first cell phone when I was 25. I know you don't really understand it, but you're just going to have to trust me."

Sometimes I feel sorry that she had a childhood in the dark ages, and I've told her that.

She doesn't feel the same way about it.

"I may not have had cell phones and internet, but I also don't have people snapping random pictures and sharing them on social media. See Thomas, I did dumb things when I was a kid, too. The difference between you and I is that mine wasn't recorded on an iPhone for all eternity."

I guess there's that.

So, I was careful with Kat, meticulous, and to this day I have never given her any personal information other than my first name.

If only that had been good enough.

Katastrophe1721 - *Thomas, have you got a minute?*

TheBestThomas - Hey Kat! Yeah, sure! What's up?

Katastrophe1721 - *I wanted to talk to you about your dream. You know the one where you thought you pulled a character out of the game?*

TheBestThomas - Ha! Yeah, I forgot I told you about that. It sure was a weird dream!

Katastrophe1721 - *What if I told you that it wasn't a dream?*

TheBestThomas - ......

Katastrophe1721 - *I know, it's a lot to think about, but I'm just asking you to keep an open mind, okay?*

TheBestThomas - Uh....okay.....

Katastrophe1721 - *Can you meet me in Soro's tonight, around 11 p.m.?*

TheBestThomas - Yeah, but why?

Katastrophe1721 - *I just want to show you something, promise! It'll be painless!*

TheBestThomas - Okaaaaaay.....

Katastrophe1721 - *See you then!*

That was it, that was the extent of the conversation that started it all.

I don't blame myself though, I mean maybe it would have taken her longer to find an "in" if I hadn't talked to her about my dream, but eventually, she'd have found a way.

If not her, then someone else. Believe me when I say that someone else would have been much, much worse.

At least with Kat, I had a chance to come to terms with things.

More than that, I had a chance to learn how to use my ability, to learn how to defend myself.

At the time of the conversation, it was only around 8 p.m., so I had a lot of time to kill before I needed to log on and meet her.

My mind was going a mile a minute trying to figure out what she could want.

We'd had so many in-game conversations by this time, the way she worded her request was setting off my alarm bells.

I tried to play some "Awesome Little Green Men" with Jed, but it was hard to concentrate, and he just ended up annoying me.

Which makes me think of something else I wanted to say.

That whole thing with Jed telling you that I'd changed, that something big must be going on, etc.

It's not true.

I mean it's true that something big is going on, but at the time I had no idea how big it was, so that wasn't a factor.

The fact of the matter is that I'm almost 13, Jed is 10, and he IS annoying.

He's always in my business, always in my room, always wanting to be the center of attention.

I think it must come from him being the baby in the family?

Not only was he the baby, but mom knew he was the last kid, so she coddled him like crazy. For the first 8 years of his life he could do no wrong, and by the time she realized what kind of a monster she'd created, he was well and truly established.

Don't get me wrong, she's got him on the straight and narrow now, but it doesn't mean he's just abandoned all the annoying habits.

If he doesn't get his way, he yells, like at the top of his lungs. And while mom and dad hate this and deal with it, I still have to hear it before they step in.

If we play games together, like "war" out in the yard, he always has to win. No matter what imaginary weapon I have, his is better. If I've got a super nuke, he's got a super-duper nuke, etc. If I win, he loses his ever-loving mind.

To say the child has a hot temper is an understatement.

So, while I appreciate his good intentions, I really do, Roblox had nothing to do with why I'd been surly toward him.

Don't tell him that, though.

Anyhow, when I left him yelling about me beating him in our little green men war, I ended up back in my room, trying to read a book. After staring at the page long enough for my Kindle to shut off, I knew I wouldn't be getting anything done until I met up with Kat.

What is she going to tell me?

My mind wanders back to the dreams I have. They do seem very real. I can reach right through my screen, into the game. After the dream where the little guy was gesturing to me, I've never had another like it, but I have done all sorts of other things in there. I've moved players around, broken off chunks of buildings, tossed cars off of bridges.

It's sort of like being King Kong, lol.

I shift on my bed so that I can reach the floor. My fingers brush the little action figure tucked under the wood lip of my bed frame, and I pick him up, examining his tiny, perfect features.

It gives me a sick sort of feeling in my stomach.

Chapter 3

Eleven o'clock finally rolls around, and I log in to the game. Kat's already on, she's hanging out at Soro's, so I click on her controller icon to join that world.

My character spawns at the restaurant, and I get an option to work. I click the button that says I'm off duty, then I go and sit at a table.

I don't know why I sit at a table, I'm already sitting at my desk, it's not like I'm standing around talking to her, but it feels like the right thing to do, so I just roll with it.

Pretty much as soon as I'm in, my chat bar lights up with a message:

Katastrophe1721 - *Hey, Thomas! Can you put on your headset so we can chat?*

TheBestThomas - Yep! Give me a sec.

This isn't a new thing, we both have accounts with Discord, so we just log in and join the same channel.

"Hey Kat! Can you hear me?"

"I hear ya! How are you?"

"Well, I'm a little freaked out about all of this, but other than that, I'm good!"

I wait for her to say something reassuring, something to let me know this conversation isn't going to be the big deal I think it's going to be, but she doesn't.

"Unfortunately, I think I'm going to freak you out even more in a moment, so prepare yourself."

I take my hand off my mouse and cross my arms in front of me, leaning back in my chair, unsure of what to say.

I settle for making light of it.

"Alright! I'll try! Hit me with your best shot!"

"Oh, I will!" She walks away from me in the game. "Can you meet me in the kitchen?"

The restaurant is set up just like I imagine any real restaurant would be. You enter through a set of double glass and wood doors, there's an entryway with a little bit of bench seating set along either side, just in case there's a wait.

The dining room is immediately beyond this, separated into two sides by an enormous aquarium filled with brightly colored fish and coral. The aquarium is actually a huge oval, so the two sections of the dining room share floor space in the very front and in the very back.

In the back, there's a single metal door with a circle shaped window in the top. The door swings both ways, so it's easy for waiters to push it open as they come in and out with trays full of food and drinks.

I get up from my seat in the dining room, walk past the aquarium on my right-hand side and head through that metal door, calling out a warning as I enter, just in case any waiters are coming through on the other side.

There's nothing like dropping an entire order of food because someone swung the door into your face. Not only does your tip suck, because it took you way too long to deliver the food, but you have to pay for the food you dropped.

If you're making $5.00 an hour and you manage to drop $75.00 worth of food, that might be your whole paycheck for the week, not just the night.

Call out a warning when you come through the door, period.

As I cross the threshold of said door into the kitchen, I spot Kat.

Her little character is standing among the other occupants like she hasn't got a care in the world. I don't believe the other people in the kitchen feel the same way.

Chefs bark orders, waiters load trays, busboys carry huge tubs of dirty dishes to the sinks. It's pretty chaotic.

The chaos is only compounded because all of these people now have to walk around her.

The kitchen layout reminds me of what people call a "Galley". There are long counters on either side of the room, one section holds oven/stove combinations, another section holds cutting boards for food prep. The back houses a giant refrigerator/freezer, and beside that is the cleaning station.

Racks are attached to the ceiling, and pots hang from every available inch.

#Watch your head.

"Okay, let's start with something easy." Kat turns to face me as I come to a stop next to her character.

"Something easy?" I'm totally not understanding what she means.

Instead of answering, she walks beneath one of the hanging racks, reaches up, and grabs a large noodle pot from above her head. It's the type of pot that would hold enough water and spaghetti to make pasta for everyone on your block.

She takes the pot across the kitchen to one of the large sinks, bumping waiters out of her way as she goes. She's really disrupting stuff in here, and I feel sorry for all the people trying to do their jobs.

Lifting the pot into the sink, she sets it under the tap, twists the faucet to full blast, and fills the pot with water. When it gets to the very brim, she picks it up (which she totally would not be able to do in real life cause that thing would be so heavy) and heads to one of the stoves, sliding the pot onto a burner.

"Why are you cooking?" This makes no sense to me, I know she can cook in the game already, so how is this a big deal?

"I'm not cooking, Thomas," she says, "you are."

Now I'm even more confused.

Flipping a switch on the stove, she ignites the burner causing white tipped blue flames to lick up from beneath the curved edges of the pot.

After a few seconds, the pot starts to boil and bubble. Stuff like this happens fast in the game, nothing takes as long as it does in real life.

Kat looks around the kitchen, assessing, for what, I don't know. Then she looks at me and holds up a finger, "One more second," she says, before walking off.

At the hanging rack in the center of the kitchen, she stops and grabs another large noodle pot. This one remains empty, and she places it upside down on the counter right next to the pot bubbling on the stove.

Finally, she goes over to one of the enormous cupboards that house all of the non-perishable items, grabs a box of spaghetti, and places it on top of the pot she just put on the counter.

Finished with whatever it is she's doing, she brushes her hands together and turns to me. "Okay, done. Now all I want you to do is tip the box of spaghetti into the pot."

Well, that's easy enough. I still don't see what the big deal is.

"Alright...." I tell her, as I walk over to the pot and start clicking around, trying to figure out how to interact with the box of spaghetti.

She frowns at me, which is a pretty horrible expression on a digital character, if you were wondering.

"I can't mess with it. What button am I supposed to push?"

Her expression goes from irritated to thoroughly exasperated.

"No, Thomas," she says, sharply! "Reach into the screen and tip the box with your finger."

Chapter 4

I sit there for a minute, silent, not really sure how I'm supposed to respond to that request. Then it hits me, this is about my dreams!

"Kat," I say in a voice I might use to speak to a mental patient, "I know I told you about my dream, but it was just a dream. People don't reach into computer screens."

She's silent for a minute, and I have this bizarre hope that she might let it go, but then she says. "Okay, let's approach this from a different direction."

As the pot continues to bubble on the stove, Kat moves away. "Stay here, I'll be right back."

I stand there, then decide to turn off the stove. You can cause fires in this game and it's a giant pain in the butt when it happens. All the food burns right down the countertop. You have to rush around to find a fire extinguisher, and there's a good chance the restaurant will clear out, meaning you lose out on tips and wages.

Turning off the burner is easy, I just click a button in the game and the blue flames disappear, easy peasy.

Around this time, Kat comes back into view. She takes the pot off the stove and dumps the hot water in the sink, leaving the pot in the sink, tipped upside down. Then she takes the upside down pot off the countertop, brings it to the sink, and fills it with water.

Apparently, she wanted a pot of water, but not a pot of hot water.

She places this newly filled pot on the very edge of the countertop.

Next, she heads to the back of the kitchen where the freezer and dishwashing station is. There's also a large pantry with a set of double wooden doors. I've been in there before, so I know what it contains.

Napkins, tablecloths, and aprons take up one side of shelves. The other side is packed with things that can't be reused, like paper towels, toothpicks, and wooden chopsticks in little paper packets.

Kat bypasses the linens and tablecloths, instead reaching to the non-reusable shelf. She grabs a whole roll of paper towels and a box of wooden chopsticks. Bringing both back to where I'm standing, she squats down on the floor about 2 feet in front of the countertop, just below where the pot of water sits.

One by one, she rips the paper towels off the roll and places them on the floor, making a fluffy pile of 10 sections. Once that's done, she grabs a packet of chopsticks, rips the paper open with her teeth, pulls out the chopsticks, and lays them on the floor beside her.

She continues in this manner until she has a half dozen individual chopsticks, then she starts placing them on their ends, resting against each other in a teepee formation on top of the paper towels.

Finally, she adds more paper towels all around the outside of the teepee, leaving one side open.

When she finishes, it's basically a mound of paper towels and chopsticks sitting on the floor right below where she put the pot of water.

I start to get a bad feeling.....

"Kat, what are you going to do?"

It takes her a minute to reply, but when she does, it's not what I want to hear. "I'm giving you a sense of urgency."

In quick motions, she pulls the rest of the paper towels off the roll, setting them aside. Then she picks up the paper towel tube, brings it over to the stove, turns on the burner, lights the tube, and shoves it underneath the chopstick teepee.

WHOOSH

Almost instantly, the paper towel teepee goes up in flames!

I don't know whether to be bothered or concerned. Bothered because she's lit a fire in the restaurant, or concerned because she really thinks this is accomplishing something.

And there it is, that moment when I look at this person I've known for months online and think.....she might be crazy.

I should have listened to my mom better.

The characters in the game think it's accomplishing something, for sure though, and I decide to feel bothered. I mean, these are kids, most likely, and they're working here trying to earn money to buy one thing or another.

I know how it feels to really want something in the game. It can take hours and hours of effort to earn enough to afford whatever it is.

Kat is totally screwing that up. These kids aren't going to get paid for the night, the customers are going to leave, and while Roblox will reset at midnight, repairing any damage, it's still not very friendly.

"Kat," I say, "what the heck, dude? That was completely uncool of you."

"Well, I guess you better fix it then," she replies, coolly.

As the fire spreads and builds, the staff in the kitchen go into rescue mode.

One of the waiters runs toward the fire extinguisher, intent on putting the fire out before it has a chance to spread. There's a little clock in the center of my screen now. It's counting down from 30, indicating the staff on duty have less than a minute to put the fire out, or the restaurant will shut down until the world resets.

Before the waiter has a chance to reach the fire extinguisher, it disappears. Just *poof*, gone.

What the heck?

"Better hurry, Thomas," Kat chides.

Did she have something to do with that extinguisher?

The waiter who was headed toward it turns in confused circles, looking around like maybe he'll find it elsewhere. He won't though, there's only one in the kitchen.

The fire is blazing in the center of the floor now, the air conditioning beginning to shift the paper towels, inching them ever closer to the pile of discarded trash Kat left nearby. If the fire reaches that spot, there's no way this fire will slow down, it'll probably engulf the entire restaurant.

Characters run into the kitchen to see what is going on as chefs and waitstaff run in the opposite direction, creating a gnarled traffic jam at the double swinging door.

The chat bar is going crazy with people asking what in the heck she is doing.

"Put it out!"

"What are you doing?!"

"You're ruining the world!"

"Good going! I'm not going to get paid!"

Kat just stands there, backing up once in awhile to get away from the flames.

"Are you ready to put out the fire, Thomas?"

The flames are spreading even faster now, black smoke is filling the screen, and people are running around like mad.

I'm getting kind of irritated with her. I mean, whatever she's doing, she's ruining a game that someone else worked hard to build, and that makes me mad.

"Kat, stop it! You're being ridiculous, and someone is going to have to fix all of this!"

"You can stop it, Thomas. Just push the water over. If you don't, Soro's is going to burn to the ground, all because you didn't do anything to help."

How can she treat someone else's hard work so disrespectfully. Does she not realize how many hours of work it takes to design a game?

I want to reach through that screen and flick her little character into the next room!

So I do.

Chapter 5

I have about 3 seconds where I think, *"Man, that was awesome!"*

It felt so good to flick her across the restaurant! I really enjoyed seeing her arms and legs burst apart from her torso, it was so satisfying!

Then I snap back to reality, errr, virtual reality. Kat is definitely not in the game, but she'll respawn soon enough. The restaurant is STILL on fire, and it's spreading rapidly toward the trash pile.

The counter on the screen counts down.

17

16

15

14

The kitchen is in chaos, none of the characters seem to know what to do. I click frantically on the pot of water, trying to dump it, but it doesn't work.

Suspending my sense of "This isn't really happening", I reach back into the screen, grasp the pot of water, and pour it onto the inferno.

There's a hiss, a billowing cloud of thick grey smoke, and the fire is out. The counter on my screen fades away, as though it was never there.

I pull my hand out of the screen and hold it up in front of my face, staring at my fingers. The same as they were 30 seconds ago, and yet so completely different.

I wiggle them, waiting for lightning or smoke to *pffft* from their tips. That doesn't happen, of course, but still....

"Awwwwweeeesooooommmeeee," I say.

It really is.

Kat's character blinks back into the game, arms and legs reattaching to her body in some kind of morbid bungee effect. She stands in front of me, angry frown replaced by a brilliant grin.

"She's proud of me," I think to myself, "proud and something else."

I can't describe the look on her face. She's happy, but she's also smug like she officially knows something I don't know.

What's that saying? "Hindsight is 20/20".

Indeed, it is. But that's a story for another day.

"Kat! Are you okay?" I almost shout it when I see her, I feel so guilty. "Ohmygoodnessiamsosorry!" It comes out all in a rush.

"I'm fine, Thomas!" She sounds so happy, she's almost giddy. "You did so well, wow!"

She's manic, pacing, hopping. "I mean, I already suspected you were a Jumper, but I have never seen anyone Jump like that, it was incredible!"

"A Jumper? What's a Jumper?"

"In a nutshell," she says, "it's someone who can venture into Roblox in one form or another."

Wow, so there's more than just me that can do this, I guess.

"We can't all do what you can do." She's oblivious to my train of thought. "Some of us can come bodily into the game via portals, some of us can modify the game just by thinking about it, and some of us....well, really it's all too unbelievable to explain accurately."

Unbelievable is right.

"You'll find out more as you meet more people like you." She turns to look at the damage her fire caused. It bothers me, watching her survey the damage. It's a lot of damage, too. It didn't shut the place down, but it was a near thing.

It occurs to me how ruthless she is.

Yes, this was a digital world, but it wasn't her world, she didn't create it. But she destroyed it, without even blinking, she destroyed it.

What else would she destroy to reach her end goal?

I think these thoughts now, not then.

Too late.

What I do think is, "More people like me? I'm not actually sure I want to know more people like me.", but I keep those thoughts to myself.

"Okay, so your little experiment worked. What was the point of it?"

"The point is that there's something else I need you to do for me in this game." She looks around the room. "I don't have a bunch of time to explain it all, but what you need to know is that you REALLY do not like playing "Soro's" at all."

"What?" I'm incredulous. This is my favorite game! I spent weeks brushing up on my grammar and punctuation so I could ace the interview. Of course, I like playing it, else I wouldn't be here, would I?

"What do you mean I don't like Soro's? I'm in it all the time, it's like one of my FAVORITE games!"

"Okay, Thomas, so let me get this right," she says, with a bit of a sarcastic bite to her voice. "You love a game about cooking, serving, and hosting more than any other game you've ever played in Roblox. Is that right?"

"Yeah, I mean it's just totally awesome!"

Only, when I say that.....it doesn't feel right.

"Alright," Kat says "When did you start loving Soro's so much?"

I have to think about it. "Uhmmmm, maybe.....I don't know, a month ago?"

"That makes total sense," she nods as if confirming a theory.

"I don't follow," I say.

"What if I were to tell you that about a month ago, I have it on very good authority that a technology company paid a Jumper to come into this game carrying a beacon, and that beacon gives off a signal that makes Soro's the perfect game for EVERYONE playing it."

"Pfft, what? Are you for real? That's not even possible." I can't even entertain the idea, it's crazy!

"It is possible, and what's more, it's exactly why you like this game so much. Listen, Thomas. Do this thing for me, and I will prove to you that what I'm saying is true." She gestures around the room, "Help me get the beacon out of the game, and you'll see that the moment it's gone, you will be completely over anything to do with Soro's."

I don't believe her at all, it's just so absurd, but she was right about me reaching into the game, so I decide to go ahead and give her the benefit of the doubt.

"Do I just have to do something like I just did?" I need to clarify this before we start. "Just reach into the game, nothing else?"

"Yes. All I need is your hands, I'll take care of the rest."

What could it hurt? I mean if something goes wrong, I just take my hand out, right?

"Alright, Kat...." I say, "I'll do it, but if it is anything more than what you're telling me, don't expect me to stick around."

"Awesome!" She walks off, fully expecting me to follow. "Let's get started."

And just like that, Kat and I became a team.

Chapter 6

"Okay." Kat and I are walking out of Soro's. She's still issuing orders. "Follow me. Before we get started, there's something I want to try."

I click around on my keys, making my little dude walk behind her, out of the restaurant, and into the parking lot, where she hangs a right behind the building, leading me to a pretty empty back lot.

There's nothing back here except a dumpster, as far as I can tell.

"What is it? Why are we back here?" I'm a little worried she's going to set my house on fire, or something. I mean "haha", not really, but....yeah, sort of.

"I want to see how many different ways you can interact with Roblox."

Do the what?

"What do you mean?" I have no idea what she means.

"Like, is it just your hands or whatever you can fit through your Mac screen," she elaborates, "or could you come all the way into the game if I made you a portal?"

"A portal?" I am so confused. "What's a portal?"

I know what a portal is, I'm not dumb, but I need to know what she means by "portal". If she's about to experiment on me in a way that might take me even more into Roblox, I think I'm probably not on board with that.

"So….I can create a large portal in your room, and then you're going to try to walk through it. If you make it through, you would end up in this world, your whole body."

Yeah, see, that's what I thought she meant.

"I'm actually not sure I want to do that at all." But even as I speak, I can feel myself wavering. How cool would it be to go INSIDE of a video game?

Really cool.

"If I can make it through, can you send me back out right away?" I have no willpower.

"I can," she says, getting excited. "I know where the portal in this game is, and I know you have to be in top management to get in the room. Lucky for you, I am!"

Yes, lucky for me. I can describe how I feel right now with MANY different words, but lucky would not be one of them.

I keep that to myself.

"Alright, so how do you do it? I'm not saying I'll go, I'm just asking for more information."

She isn't deterred, maybe she can sense my weakness. "It's easy! I'm going to need a focal point though, so you're going to need to pick something in your room that I can use to anchor the portal."

I look around my room, it's messy, Jed is right about that....

My eyes land on a Redstone Block that my mom gave me for Christmas two years ago. I'm not actually sure that it works anymore, but it's worth a shot.

I scoot my chair back and grab the block off my shelf. "How about this?" I hold the block up to the screen.

Then it occurs to me that maybe she can't see me through the screen.

Actually, how creepy would it be if she COULD see me through the screen? I've been playing Roblox with her for months!

I try to think back in my head to all of the things I did while playing with her.

Ohhhh Gosh.....

The list is really endless.

Did I pick my nose? Did I fart? Did I wear CLOTHES all the time?

This could be really awful. My face turns beet red, and I swallow hard.

"Kat, can you see me right now?" PLEASE don't let her be able to see me!

"No." She's oblivious to the panic attack I've just had. "If you'll turn on your camera, I'll be able to see you. Otherwise, I can only see your in-game character."

Oh, thank goodness!

"So you can't even see my hands when I push them through the screen?" I was wondering about that, wondering what the other characters saw on their screens.

"Nope! To me, it just looked like a pot of water tipping over."

I think about when I flicked her, and she seems to be thinking about the same thing.

"When you pushed me though, It totally affected my character, so be careful."

Says the lady who set a restaurant on fire.

"Alright, I will, and I'll turn my camera on, give me a sec."

I toggle out of my screen and turn on my camera. The light on top of my computer blinks to life, then glows a soft green, letting me know I'm live and in color.

"Hey!" Kat's character raises an arm and waves to me.

I'm a bit confused because I thought she'd be turning on her camera as well so I could see her, but I guess not.

"Hey yourself!" I wave as well, for good measure.

Chapter 7

Now that she can see me, I hold up the Redstone Block again, "How's this?".

She responds right away, "Perfect, put it on the floor out of the way a bit."

Getting out of my chair, I scan my room, then decide to place it at the base of the emptiest wall. I don't know much of anything about mystical portals, but it seems like it might need a little elbow room.

The baseboard juts out from the wall about an inch, so I just set the block right there in front of it.

Back at my computer, I put my headset on and let Kat know that I'm ready. "Alright," I tell her, "do your worst!"

It's a joke, but now that I think about it, maybe it's a lousy joke....

"Kat, you're not going to light anything on fire or anything, right?"

"No, silly, what a dumb question! I'm just going to open a portal, and then I'm going to ask you to walk through it. Easy Peasy."

Well, when she puts it like that.

"Okay, but you can send me RIGHT BACK if I go through, right? I do NOT want to be in the game, not at all, no desire to do so, none!" I'm adamant.

"Yes, if you make it through, I'll say hello, and then I'll have you walk right back out." She sounds sincere, but she seemed sincere through this whole thing, not at all like someone who would take drastic action, not at all like someone who would lure my little brother into things.

I didn't know about that at the time, though.

"Alright, I'll do it." I glance over at the block like it's going to explode or something.

She's silent for a few seconds, and then she crackles back to life in my headset.

"Great. All you need to do is tap the block 3 times, and the portal should pop up right in front of you."

Well, here goes nothing. I get up and walk hesitantly back to the block then squat down again. I'm sort of sitting on my feet, but with my legs bent (so I can run away really fast if I need to). I stretch out my arm as far as it will go, only touching the Redstone Block with the very tips of my fingers.

Sucking in a deep breath, I do it quickly, like taking that awful medicine mom gave me when our whole family got bronchitis.

tap tap tap

The block glows red, and the portal does indeed pop up right away. It's this crazy looking blue-ish silver swirly thing straight out of a science fiction movie.

"Perfect! Now go ahead and walk through."

I stand up, ignoring the tingling feeling of blood rushing back into my legs, and approach the portal in the same manner I approached tapping the block.

Quickly.

I power walk toward the portal, I'm ready to do this thing, no matter what's on the other side, I'm going to meet it head on!

SMACK

That's me meeting it head-on.

Ouch.

"Well, that answers that question," Kat says, "no portals for you."

I rub my forehead and my nose.

"No, I guess not."

Chapter 8

"Okay, we know you can't use the portals, and we know you can touch items and people in the game. What we need now," she continues, "is a game plan."

"Maybe if you clue me in on what we're doing, I might be able to help."

"You already know about the beacon, I told you that much." she replies. "In a nutshell, I have to find the beacon, and then I have to find someone to remove it from the game."

"Can I remove the beacon through my screen? Like if you were to hand it to me." It sounds pretty reasonable. I mean we've established that I can remove things, so why not this beacon she's talking about?

"I'm not sure," she says. "That's sort of what I was thinking as well, though."

"So where is the beacon? How do we find it?"

Frankly, most of the worlds in Roblox are quite large, and if she doesn't have an idea of where to find this thing, we could be looking for a very long time.

"I don't know exactly where it is," she tells me, "but I do know that most of the time, the beacons are placed in a spot that players would not accidentally stumble upon."

What I find out when I get home is that this is true.

Jed got a beacon out of the guard barracks in Prison Life, and out of the captain's quarters in Zombie Assault. Those are most definitely places most players would not go.

"That makes sense. So in a game like this, we know that most players are going to have easy access to the restaurant, the kitchen, the employee lounge, the parking lot....anything I'm missing?"

"No, that sounds about right," she agrees.

"Keeping that in mind," I tell her, "it sounds like the place with the least chance of accidental interaction would be somewhere that only management can go. Right?"

"Right," she confirms.

"Well, you're management, Kat, so where do you go that no one else can go?"

She's quiet for a bit, I guess she's going through the possibilities in her head.

"I can go to the management lounge, but that seems like a poor choice because really there are a lot of people in management," she tells me.

"What about someplace you wouldn't be able to go regularly, but maybe you'd be able to go with permission." I'm just throwing ideas out there. "Is there some sort of management training site? Or what about a retreat?"

I remember my mom going on company gatherings a few times. She'd head out of state for a few days to hang out with the other people in her company.

"No, nothing like that," Kat says.

"Okay, well what about a party? Does your founder, creator....I have no idea what to call him. Do they have like a Christmas party?"

It's not that close to Christmas, but it is December, and I know that a lot of companies host their parties early in the year so as not to interfere with other stuff families might want to do.

Does the same stuff happen in Roblox? I have no idea.

"Yes," Kat says, triumphant! "Great idea, Thomas! There is a holiday party coming up, it's at the boss's house in the game, and I would imagine very few people get a chance to wander around that place."

"It sounds to me like the perfect place to keep a beacon." I'm getting excited about this all of the sudden! "So, what do we do, how do we get in?"

"I'm going to need to think on that," she says. "I mean, it would be for management, you are definitely NOT management, and you'd have to be there as well to help me with this."

She's right.

"There has to be a way though," I tell her. "So this guy throws a huge party, he invites the top management, but he needs help right?"

At that moment, I know I've landed on a great idea!

"Help! That's it! He's going to need wait staff to walk around serving his snooty little finger foods and fancy drinks, so why not hire waiters who are already working at Soro's?"

It's brilliant! I've already passed their vetting process, they know I'm more than capable of acting professionally and using proper grammar, which I'm sure they'll want on display in their wait staff.

"That is a great idea, Thomas," Kat exclaims! "Let me work on this, I'll talk to the owner and throw it out as a suggestion. I just know he'll go for it!"

"Awesome!" Though really, why I'm excited about playing waiter, I'm not sure.

"Get some sleep," she says to me. "I'll have more information for you tomorrow, and we can put our plan into action."

I look at the clock, it's pretty late, after midnight, and I realize that I really am tired.

"Alright, night Kat."

Shutting my laptop, I remove the headset and scoot away from the desk.

Never in my life did I think I'd be so excited about a Roblox Christmas party.

Chapter 9

Did I say I was excited?

Scratch that!

I'm so nervous, I could puke.

Actually, I wouldn't dare puke right now. If I did, it would get all over the front of my waitering tuxedo. I'd have to leave the party, at least long enough to log out and change clothes, then my manager would kill me. He might not let me back into the party at all, and Kat would be on her own.

Then she'd kill me.

All the killing aside, I have to think about the amount of Robux I had to spend on this monkey suit! Do you know how much it costs to buy a tuxedo in Roblox? Go look it up.

Note to self: Someone needs to create an "outfit rental" Roblox store. Like where I can pay you 5 Robux and wear my choice of outfit for 24 hours, or something.

That's really a great idea.

"Thomas, head in the game!" I turn to see who's talking to me.

It's my manager, his name is "DaManInCharge2007". Apparently, he's been gunning for some sort of promotion at Soro's, and if he pulls this party off without a hitch, he'll have a much better chance.

"Yes, sir." If there were a Roblox "/eyeroll" emote, I'd be turning my back to him and doing it!

I so would.

I say that I "responded", but you need to remember that I'm not in the game. I'm sitting at my computer, maneuvering my little character all over a house, where other characters are standing around.

The chat bar is going crazy, and I can only keep track of people talking to me when they send me a private message.

Otherwise, I'm pretty much just typing in "Would you like some more champagne?" or "Have you tried the delicious cream cheese salmon rolls?"

It's rather mind-numbing.

My little guy is all dressed up in his overpriced tuxedo, looking quite sharp for a bunch of mashed together pixels if I do say so myself.

I haven't seen Kat yet, but I know she'll be here. We went over the plan about 52 times in the last 12 hours, so I'm not worried at all about her doing her part.

My part, though. I can't think about it too much, or the puking feeling comes back with a vengeance.

Basically, Kat and I are supposed to search the house.

No, that doesn't sound dramatic enough.

Kat and I are supposed to search this GIANT house while HUNDREDS of people walk around.

Also, Kat is pretty sure there's going to be another Jumper here. One who's on the payroll of "The Company" and will be keeping an eye out.

Yeah, I know all about them, too.

No pressure.

I've already scoped out the downstairs area, let me give you the layout, so you understand.

You enter through the front door (well I didn't, cause I'm just "the help"), and that leads into a vast entryway. Once there, you can see the two colossal curving staircases on either side that lead to the second floor.

If you go straight into the entryway, you'll come to a large living area, which is where the party is mainly being held.

From there, you see two doors leading out of the living room, one on each side. The door on the right leads to the dining room, the door on the left goes to the game room.

If you go into the dining room, you can take another door to the kitchen, and from the kitchen, you can go out the back door.

The game room is also full of people, mingling, eating, and having fun. This room has a pool table, a huge TV, stand up video games, etc.

You can exit that room only one way, into a hallway that has a bathroom, and then leads back to the entry.

The game room is where I am now, walking among the guests, offering my cheese and "champagne".

It's not really champagne, okay? It's sparkling apple juice.

When the average player is 12 years old, you can't be serving alcohol.

I thought you knew that.

Every time I walk into this room with fresh trays of stuff, it makes me laugh. I mean who puts a video game INSIDE of a video game?

People with too much time on their hands, that's who.

Little Roblox characters are lined up at the video game stations, though. They're playing Pac-Man or Galaga or who knows what. I kind of want to try one the games myself, just to see.

I mean, does the screen replace my computer screen, or will I be squinting down at this tiny arcade game?

#thingsineedtoknow

It's in this room that I first spot Kat, and I almost don't recognize her!

She is also dressed differently, very formal and fancy in a dark blue dress and some ornate hat with feathers all over it. The dress is paired with elbow length gloves and sparkling gold jewelry.

#ladeeda

Walking near the crowd she's talking to, I continue my "Champagne? Cream cheese salmon roll?" drill.

Kat catches my eye, then takes a salmon roll off my tray before turning back to her "friends". I think she's going to ignore me, and I'm about ready to walk off when she "accidentally" drops it on to her dress.

"Oh my gosh! Look what I've done! I am so clumsy!" She cries out. It's really believable!

The people in the group utter shocked exclamations. "Oh no!", "I hope it won't stain!", and stuff like that.

Like, really? This is pixels, people! I guess it's more fun when you really get into it, though.

"Madam," I say, holding out my arm, "please let me show you to a room where you can clean that from your dress."

"Oh, thank you so much," she effuses.

We're really naturals at this spy stuff.

I lead her out of the gaming room, down a hallway, and to a bathroom. She enters the bathroom, shutting the door, and I walk off, but not really.

Once I get to the stairway, I walk beneath the curve, putting my tray down on the floor, and pushing it deep into the shadows, so it doesn't get kicked over.

Now that I'm out of sight, I wait, but not for very long.

A few minutes later, just enough time for anyone to think that we've gone our separate ways, Kat comes out of the bathroom and joins me at the staircase. She's still wearing the blue dress and jewelry, but the giant chicken is gone from her head.

"You took off your feather hat."

I was kind of wondering how she was going to search in that thing, it was huge!

"Yeah, it was VERY in the way. I just left it in the bathroom." She smirks. "It's sitting on the back of the toilet like some kind of feathered object de art."

"Good idea. You'd have a hard time blending in or ducking for cover!" I laugh.

"Very funny. Enough joking around, we've got work to do." She grabs my arm, and we head toward the second floor.

It's time to find that beacon.

Chapter 10

I remember reading somewhere once that if you want to go somewhere you aren't supposed to be, you should act like you belong there. With that in mind, Kat and I walk up the stairs like we own the place.

Calm stride, shoulders back, no looking over our shoulders to see if anyone is watching us. If asked, we'll just say we couldn't find the downstairs bathroom, so we went upstairs to see if we could find one there.

We decided on the second floor because we both had full access to the first floor over the last couple of hours, but we didn't see anything.

Of course, there's a chance it's still there somewhere, but Kat thinks the second floor is a better bet since it'll have an even more limited amount of people with access.

"How are we going to find this thing?"

We've been over the plan a bunch, but we still kind of have to rely on luck to locate the beacon. All I know about it FOR SURE is that it will glow.

We've looked at the blueprints, so we know the layout of the upstairs area. The top floor is basically one long hallway with doors on either side. You can go right at the stair or left at the stairs, but no matter which way you choose, it's a long hallway.

We decide to split up, one of us will start at one end, the other will begin at the other end, and we'll make our way back to the middle, hopefully with the beacon.

"I have nothing new to add to the plan. Just remember to turn off the lights as soon as you get in the room. If there are open curtains, shut them. Make it as dark as you can, and that'll give you a better chance to see the glow."

"Got it," I keep my voice to a whisper.

Kat goes left, I go right.

I continue all the way down to the end of the hall. There are 2 doors on the right, and 2 doors on the left. I decide to start on the right at the last room, cross the hall, and then go back, so I'm making a sort of a zig-zag motion.

The first door I come to is a bedroom, apparently a guest room based on its sterile appearance. There's nothing in here to indicate that anyone lives in this place full time.

Do people actually live full time in a Roblox house?

Probably not, right? So maybe all of the rooms will look like this?

It's already dark outside, but I go ahead and close the curtains anyway, just to be sure I'm making it as dark as possible. Then I go to each door in the room and open it.

The first leads to an en-suite bathroom, which is great because I really have to pee. I close the door, do my business, wash my hands, and continue on with the search.

The second door leads to a closet, so I leave the light off and leave the door open, same as the bathroom.

Once that's done, I go back to the light switch and turn off the light, then I stand still for a minute, so my eyes adjust before looking around.

Nothing, no glow anywhere.

For good measure, I check under the bed, stuff like that, but still, I see no glow.

I put the room back in order, shut the door, and move across the hall to the furthest room on the left. I do the same thing in here, and come up with the same results.

No beacon.

Moving back across the hallway, I hit the first room on the right, it's a bathroom. I almost dismiss it and head across the hall to what must be an office or bedroom, but decide to go ahead with the search.

There's a shower, a toilet, a separate tub, a small cupboard for towels and such, and another cabinet under the sink.

I open all of the doors, there aren't any windows to mess with, and turn off the light.

Almost immediately, I see a glow coming from the direction of the sink.

Huh.

I walk over to it, being careful not to bump into anything in the pitch black, and run my hands along the top.

Nothing.

I kneel down and look under the sink.

Nothing there either.

If anything, the glow is diminished when I look under the sink, so it's got to be coming from above.

Standing back up, I try twisting the sink handles.

Nothing, no water.

Hmmm, that is odd. I know for sure I saw water running in the kitchen sink when I showed up for my waitering job, and I did just use the restroom in the other room...

I back out of the bathroom and walk back to the first room I checked. In the room's bathroom, I turn the sink handles again, just to be totally sure.

Water pours out of the faucet.

"Alllriiiiight." I think to myself.

I head back to the bathroom I just left, kneel down in front of the sink, and think about this for a moment.

I can see the glow from the top of the sink, but not from the bottom, so whatever it is, it must be in the drain pipe, right?

Unfortunately, I can't interact with the pipes at all. No matter how much clicking I do, I can't loosen any nuts or anything like that.

Taking a deep breath, I reach my hand into my computer screen. My computer displays pushes in a little, then makes a slight *pop* sound, and I'm in!

I am still so freaked out by this!

Moving as gently as I can, I reach under the sink cabinet and feel for the little "U" shaped pipe. The material is flimsy under my fingertips, fragile, like I could break it with a thought.

It's a good thing, because it's exactly what I intend to do.

I put the tip of my index finger on the pipe and push.

Nothing happens, so I push a little bit harder.

"Snap!"

The top of the pipe breaks, leaving just the bottom connected, and the "U" in between those two points. If there is something in the drain, it has to be stuck in the bottom of that "U" pipe, so if I break it wrong, it could go straight down the drain, and if that happens, I would literally have to tear the house apart to find it.

The thought of destroying someone's hard work doesn't set well. The thought of trying to find this tiny, little...whatever it is in a pile of rubble also doesn't set well.

So I'm just going to be really gentle!

Putting my other hand in to the screen, I grasp the bottom of the pipe with two fingers, then I grab right above that spot with my other hand, creating a clear place that I intend for the pipe to break.

"Gently, Thomas. Gently like a baby deer nuzzling your cheek." Not that I know what that would feel like, but I imagine it would be gentle.

"Snap!"

It works.

#BeTheBabyDeer

Still holding the pipe, I bring my hands back out of the screen.

My left hand comes through, no problem, but my right hand, the hand holding the pipe, is stuck fast in Roblox.

Chapter 11

"Shoot!" I sit at my desk staring at my now pixelated hand on the other side of the screen.

It's just weird.

"What's the matter," Kat asks, "what's going on?"

I forgot we were still hooked up through our headsets so we could talk without typing in the game.

"I found the beacon. Or at least I found the thing the beacon is in."

"That's great! Where are you? I'll head your way."

"I'm in the bathroom, first door on the right, on my side of the hallway."

"I'm coming now, give me a sec."

In no time at all, I see the bathroom door open, and the light flips on. Kat stands there, a shocked look on her face.

"Wooooooowwwww."

"What? What's going on?!" I try to toggle my view of the screen so I can see all around, but I can't move it with my hand stuck in the game.

"I know what you can do, but it's still so odd to walk in here and see a piece of a....sink, is that a drain pipe? Anyhow, it's just floating in the middle of the bathroom. It's very odd."

It sounds cool, actually. I'd like to see it!

"Can you take a screenshot?"

"There's no time for that, you'll just have to take my word for it." She shoots me a look that tells me I need to get back on track.

"Oh fine, whatever." I mean there's always time for a screenshot.

"Well, I'm glad you're entertained," I say, "but I'm stuck here. I can't get my hand out of the screen."

"Hmmmm, clearly you're going to have to let go of the pipe. Whatever you are able to do in the game, you're not able to bring anything out with you. That's very good to know."

"Well wait, what about the action figure? I took him out of the game."

She's silent for a few seconds, thinking.

"I believe, though I have no evidence, that beacons aren't like the rest of the things in the game. It's not something the game makers created, so you can't interact with it in the same way."

"That makes no sense, you know that, right?"

"It makes sense, Thomas, and when we have more time, I'll tell you exactly why it makes sense, but for now, we need to get the beacon by itself."

"Okay, well I'm going to drop the pipe, but whatever is inside of it, it's really tiny, so please don't lose it."

"Hang on one second, bring it over to the bathtub."

I move my hand a few inches until my thumb and forefinger are hovering over the large, porcelain basin.

She takes a towel off of a hook on the wall and lays it down in the tub. She also puts the plug in the bathtub for good measure.

"Alright, go ahead and drop it." She looks up at me, expectantly, hands on her hips.

Putting my fingers as close to the tub as I can get them, I drop the pipe. It lands on the towel with barely any noise.

Kat moves over to the tub, and I can see her character messing with the pipe. She picks it up, and I can hear something rattling around as she tips it this way and that way.

Putting the pipe down, she leans over the tub, running her hand over the towel she put down.

For grins, while she's doing that, I grab the pipe again and try to pull it out of the screen.

It totally works.

Kat looks up at me, smirking. "Told ya." She holds her hand up, showing me what she took out of the pipe.

"It's a ring."

"A ring?" I can see it, but I still have to ask, because, a ring???

"Yeah, just a small gold ring, something that would be easy to drop down a sink."

"So you think they did it on purpose? Weren't they worried that it might get washed away? I mean, the water doesn't work in here, and I figured it was because they were worried about it getting washed down the pipes."

Kat moves to the sink cabinet and sticks her head in, peering into the pieces of pipe left inside. She reaches her whole hand into the section that leads down into the belly of the house then makes a grunt of understanding.

"There's a screen here, some type of trap to keep something like that from happening. It looks like whoever placed the ring here did their homework."

"But even if the beacon did wash down the drain, it would still stop in Soro's, right?"

"I'm not sure, Thomas," she says. "Maybe The Company knows something we don't."

Stupid Company, stupid greedy zombie makers. "Okay, well we've got the beacon, so now what?"

"Now, we've got to get it out of the portal. I was sort of hoping you'd be able to do that by taking it out of your computer screen, but I guess that's not going to happen."

I feel defensive all of the sudden! "Sorry, Kat! I mean it's not like I planned only to be able to enter Roblox in a limited capacity!"

"I know, I know, I didn't mean it like that," she soothes. "I'm just frustrated. I've got to find a Jumper who can get this out of here for me, and I'm not sure how to do that."

I didn't think of that, but she's right. If we don't have a way to get it out of here, the game will stay the same, compromised.

Gah, that's the suck! Let's look on the bright side.

"Well, at the very least, you have the beacon now, so you can take it with you and keep it safe, right?"

There's that!

"Yes, I can, but I really don't want to. I'm not sure if The Company tracks the beacon or not, but I'd rather not find out the hard way." She moves her neck back and forth on her shoulders, like she's trying to relieve some stress.

"I guess let's just go back downstairs for a bit, so people see us, then we can leave the party with everyone else and figure it out from there."

There's certainly no point in standing around in a bathroom.

"Okay," she nods, "I guess that'll have to do for now."

We clean up as best we're able, shutting the cabinet doors, so no one will notice the damage. I have a feeling that whoever put the beacon there also checks in periodically to make sure it's still in place.

I'm hanging the towel on the rack as Kat is leaving the bathroom. She shuts the door abruptly, and I'm about to ask her what the deal is when I hear her (see her typing in chat) talking to someone.

"Oh, hey Dirk..." she says. Then her voice turns sharp. "What are you doing here?"

Who's Dirk? Why does she sound so aggravated?

Over our shared audio connection, she's frantic. "Thomas, do NOT come out of the bathroom!"

"What? What's going on?"

"This guy, Dirk, he's a Jumper, and he's NOT on our side!"

Chapter 12

"Kat, What do I do?" I'm sort of freaking out right now. I mean I know I can just log off the game whenever I want, but it feels like this might be our only chance to get the beacon out.

If Kat takes it with her, will she be safe? What will she do with it? The thought that The Company might find her really bothers me.

We just need to get the beacon through the portal and be done with it.

But how!?!? That's the most critical part of all this, and we don't know how we're going to get it done. I'm irritated all of the sudden. She really should have thought this through more.

"Just stay in the bathroom right now," she says, "I've got an idea."

Kat continues to trade veiled barbs with Dirk in the hallway outside, but I can tell that she's moving further away from the bathroom door.

That's good. Get him away so I can get the heck out of here!

"Dirk, I will never understand why you're working with these guys," I hear her say. "You used to be a super cool guy, what happened?"

What?! This is the Jumper that's working with The Company? Why would anyone do something like that?

It takes every bit of my willpower not to leave the bathroom and confront him.

"Stay in there, Thomas!" Kat is clearly reading my mind.

"You don't know me, Katrina," he spits back. "Don't even pretend like you thought I was a "cool guy" when you barely ever said two words to me in the halls."

Whoa, these two know each other in real life? Her real name is Katrina?

"Katrina," I think to myself. I like it.

Yeah, if you're wondering, I used to have a crush on her. That is VERY past tense now, VERY!

"That's not true, Dirk," Kat retorts, hotly. "I did try to talk to you! You were just so caught up in hating everyone that you couldn't even attempt to allow people to be your friend." Kat's not pulling any punches, she's mad.

"It doesn't matter now, anyway," Dirk says. "The Company is making things happen, and I'm rising up in the ranks. You think you can stop us, but you are so.totally.wrong."

Man, this guy sounds like a total jerk.

"Well guess what, Dirk? I'm going to stop them in this game, you can bet on that."

Dirk snorts like he just can't even believe she'd think such a thing was possible. "You're not stopping anything, Kat. You of all people should know how impossible it is."

Huh? Why would she know how impossible it is?

Dirk's not done though, "Whatever you try to do, remember that I'll be one step ahead of you, just like always."

"Alright, Dirk. Whatever you say." Kat practically spits the words. "Now get out of my way, because I've got some gamers to rescue."

"Where are you going?" As though she would tell him.

"To the portal, Dirk. Where else?"

Well heck, I guess she WILL tell him!

"What are you doing!?" I hiss at her through my microphone. "Why are you telling him our plans!?"

I have a fleeting worry that Kat's not telling me anything, but it's so fast that I don't pay attention to it.

I wish I had.

"Relax, Thomas. I've got a plan, and if I know Dirk, he's going to run through that portal ASAP so that he can go tell his contact at The Company what we're up to."

It takes me a minute to catch on to her meaning.

"So, you're going to have Dirk take the beacon back through the portal?"

"Exactly," she says, triumphant!

"How are you going to pull that off? He'll never do it!"

"He's not going to know he's doing it, Thomas."

There's a definite "duh" at the end of her sentence.

"When I say, I want you to create a distraction. Come out of the bathroom once Dirk and I are out of sight, and do something that will get him moving out of the house."

"Uhhh, alright...." I say. "Like what?"

"I don't know! That's your area of expertise, just do something. You've got 30 seconds to come up with a plan."

Who does she think I am, Harry Houdini?

What can I do that will clear the house? It's full of people, there must be at least 200 guests here, and she wants them all to leave?

Sure, easy, simple, nooooo problem.

#not

I wait a few seconds for her and Dirk to get down the hall, then I ease out of the bathroom, looking both ways and moving slow, just to make sure they're gone.

I'm formulating a plan in my head, but it means I need to get outside.

Further down the hall, I can see that they've taken the stairs down to the first floor, so I head down as well, wishing I still had my tray as a prop.

Once they're out of sight, I walk up through the entry, into the living area, hang a right into the dining room, and then a left into the kitchen.

The other waiters look my way, no doubt wondering where I'm going, but I don't care. Bossman, or whatever his name is, isn't around, so I'm golden.

The back door leads into the backyard, and that's just where I need to be.

First thing's first, ditch the monkey suit. I pull it off and stuff it behind a bush.

I was sweltering in that thing, especially with my regular clothes underneath!

Still, what a waste of Roblox. I'm not sure it'll still be in my inventory since I'm removing it in the game and ditching it. I'm pretty sure I'll never see it again, though.

Next up....create a diversion.

It doesn't take me long to find what I'm looking for, the main breaker box attached to the side of the house. It looks just like the one attached to my house, small, greyish white, clearly a waterproof casing for some thick wires running through the wall.

It is incredible the level of detail these people put into their worlds! I am so impressed right now!

Reaching my hand through the computer screen, I grab the wire covering, and rock it back and forth, hearing the caulk snap and pull as it comes free of the brick. When it's hanging freely, I give it one last tug and pull it off the house. Some of the wires come with it, but the main one, the thickest one, holds fast.

I slide the covering down the wires, and then grab only the thick cable still left intact, yanking as hard as I can!

BZZZT!!!!

The power in the house blinks out!

"Yay!" I actually say it out loud, then look around. I hope I didn't wake anyone. With my luck, Jed will be listening at the door.

Nothing happens though, the house is quiet.

In the game though, that's another story.

My plan totally worked.

It takes less than 5 seconds for the screaming to start.

Chapter 13

"Brilliant, Thomas! These people are running out of here as fast as they can!" Apparently Kat was still in the house when I put my plan into effect.

"Awesome! I figured they wouldn't hang around long if they couldn't see anything."

"You were right! Now, meet me on the side of the house." Kat is whispering to me over the headset, and I wonder why.

Maybe it's just the heat of the moment.

All the same, it feels like the right thing to do, so I whisper back. "Okay, I'm in the back right now, I'll be there in 3 seconds."

I see her character coming around the side of the house a few seconds later, and we stand side by side. I guess there's solidarity in groups, even when those groups are just pixels.

"So what's the plan?"

"We're going to follow Dirk. If I know that little weasel, he'll be heading toward the portal as fast as his legs can carry him."

We stand at the front corner of the house, out of sight, but still able to see the guests as they stream through the large double entry doors.

Sure enough, not 2 minutes later, we see Dirk among the group exiting the party.

"There he is," she's still whispering, for some reason.

Dirk looks around, no doubt trying to find Kat, but we duck back behind the house, and he continues on his way, oblivious to his tail.

We follow him at a distance, not super close, but close enough not to lose sight of him. Since we're in the group of people leaving the party, we're all sort of taking the same route back to Soro's.

"We need to intercept him just before he gets to the portal."

"Where is the portal?" I've never seen it, so I have no idea where we're going, and therefore have no suggestions on how we might best intercept him.

"It's in the President's office, so that's why you've never seen it," she says.

Makes sense. I'm definitely not a worker the president is going to notice, heck, I barely work enough to stay employed.

We walk back into Soro's, and I can't help but think that it's a funny looking crowd.

Everyone coming from the party is all dressed up. Some of them blink out of existence, then back in, wearing their regular clothes. Others don't really care what they work in, so the hostess is in a ballgown, and the first waiter we see is in a tux and tails.

The customers notice the oddity as well and chat scrolls by with lots of comments about how it must be some special occasion, etc.

The hostess nods at Kat as we pass, and I wonder if that's something a gamer can do, or if there are more Jumpers here than I realize.

"Follow me," Kat says, and I forget to ask her about the hostess.

We weave our way through the wait staff and kitchen staff, walking through the kitchen, which has indeed been restored to its former glory since the last game reset.

There's a door in the kitchen that leads to an area I've never been to, and as we walk through, I realize this must be where management.....manages.

The door looks simple enough, drab grey/green paint, metal. If you've seen an industrial door, you've seen this one.

Kat stands in front of it and swipes a key card.

What is it with these people and key cards? I'm over it already, give me a fingerprint machine, or maybe a retinal scanner.

Key cards are so 10 years ago.

Anyhow, she swipes the card, the reader blinks green, and the lock on the door disengages. She pulls it open, gesturing for me to go first, I guess so she can make sure it's closed after she comes in. I feel a little weird about that, unlike my brother, I do believe in "ladies first", etc.

Kat's having nothing to do with chivalry though. Placing a hand on my back, she SHOVES me through the door, then turns and tugs it closed, making sure it *clicks* into place.

What we walk in to is pure, old-fashioned, wood-paneled opulence. I look around in awe. If I had a great, great, great grandfather, and he was a member of a men's only club, this is what it would look like.

The entire room is gleaming wood. The walls are wood, the ceilings are wood, all of the chairs arranged around the room have massive wood bases, as do all of the tables set in between the chairs.

The color scheme appears to be wood, reddish brown leather, reddish brown upholstery, and cream or gold accents all over. There also a little bit of navy blue here and there.

It's all very upper class!

"What does it look like to you?"

I turn around and stare at her, unsure of what to say. What does she mean?

"What do you mean? You know what it looks like, you're in here with me," I tell her.

"Haven't you been listening to me, Thomas? I told you that the beacon makes it the perfect game for YOU." She sounds exasperated. "It's going to be different for everyone, don't you get that?"

Huh. I guess I didn't think of that, but it makes sense.

"It looks like a lot of polished wood and gold trim," I tell her.

She looks around the room, and I imagine she's trying to see what I'm seeing.

"What does it look like to you?"

"You'll see in a few minutes if all goes well," she replies.

"You mean the beacon doesn't affect you?" That has to be what she means, otherwise, she wouldn't say I'd know what it looked like once the beacon is removed, which has to be what she's implying.

She ignores my question, making a beeline for another door across the room.

We walk straight through (I think it must be a casual gathering room), and head to the door at the back. This door is also wood, and if it's possible, even shinier than the rest of the wood in the room. It's been waxed and polished to such an extent that I can see my face staring back at me.

It's unnerving.

She swipes the card again, another click, another green light, and we're in. The portal is at the back of the room, already up and activated. I can only see the portal itself though, there's nothing behind it.

"Where does it go?"

"It doesn't matter where it goes, Thomas. It only matters that it leaves the game."

"Why can't I see what's on the other side?"

"You can't use the portals, so to you, it's pretty much meaningless, just a picture in the air, if you will. You'll never be able to see where they go."

If I really stare, I can sort of make out the wall in the back of the room, but there is definitely no alternate dimension waiting to be entered.

It bothers me.

I still don't get it, I don't understand how we're going to get Dirk to take the beacon through, but I leave it be because Kat is clearly on edge about it, to begin with.

"So what do we do now?" It's been a long night, I've been sitting at my desk for almost 3 hours, and I'm starting to get sleepy.

"Now, we wait." She walks to the corner of the room that's out of sight when you enter, blocked by the open door. "We saw him leave the party, I told him where we were going, he won't be far behind, you can bet on that."

I walk to the corner of the room where she's standing, and lean against the wall for a few seconds before hitting the "X" button to make my character sit on the ground. I know he doesn't get tired, but seeing him sit makes me feel more relaxed for some odd reason.

Kat follows my lead, and together we sit in silence, me thinking about how much I'd like to go to bed, and her thinking who knows what.

I have no doubt she's planning and plotting, that's for sure.

"Thomas," Kat says sharply in my ear, "wake up!"

I jerk my head up from my desk with so much force that I tip my desk chair backward, arms flailing to try and catch myself on something before I fall.

My fingers scrabble at the edge of my desk, and I get just enough purchase to keep me upright long enough that I can lean forward, correcting my backward momentum.

"Did you fall asleep?!"

"What? No! Of course, I didn't fall asleep!" For someone who did fall asleep, I feel very insulted that she would think such a thing.

"I had to pee, I just went to the bathroom. You can't expect me to just sit here all night, Kat."

It's not true, but it's believable, and maybe it'll make her feel bad.

She goes quiet, so I figure it worked, but then I realize she's quiet because something is happening in the game.

At the door, we hear the tell-tale sound of a key card being swiped through the reader on the other side. There's a *shwip* as it's pulled through the slot, a *click* as the reader accepts the card, and then another *click* as the door lock disengages.

The door handle turns, Kat and I stand up quickly, the door opens, and in walks Dirk.

Chapter 14

Kat wastes no time, she's like a tiny ball of fury!

The moment Dirk is through the door, she kicks it shut, takes a flying leap, and tackles him to the floor. He lands on his face but starts struggling immediately. She's bigger than him, but not by much, and I know it won't be long before she loses the upper hand.

"You need to get your head on straight, Dirk," she shouts at him as he scrabbles around, trying to gain some leverage, "The Company is USING you, and you're letting them!"

Dirk isn't phased, big shocker there. He knocks Kat off of his back, rather gently, actually, and is laying on the ground on his back still looking so neat in his slacks, tucked in shirt, and tie.

He's staring up at Kat like she has lost her mind. His glasses were knocked off when she tackled him, and he looks almost vulnerable.

I actually have a moment where I feel sort of sad for him.

Then I remember that he's working with the people who are basically trying to take away the free will of kids everywhere.

Jerk.

Kat makes to tackle him again, but he slides out of the way.

"Katrina," Dirk says, "kindly get off of me, it's not very ladylike."

This just irritates Kat even more. I can see it in her eyes, she wants to beat Dirk senseless, and she's about to give in.

It's time for me to intervene.

"Kat, stop this," I say to her, "there's nothing we can do, just leave it be, we'll figure out another way."

She looks at me, and the look on her face is so raw and desperate that I think she might start crying.

I walk over to her, take her arm, and gently lift her to her feet. She comes willingly enough, and I get the feeling that if I weren't holding her up, she'd fall right back down to the ground.

"It's okay," I say to her, "it's okay, we'll figure it out."

I cannot even imagine how she's feeling. She knows Dirk can use the portals, he was her last best hope to get the beacon out of the game, and now it's too late.

She pushes her face into my shoulder, and I rub her arm. I really want to beat Dirk to a pulp right now.

He gets up off the ground slowly, walks over to his glasses, cleans them off on his shirt sleeves, and puts them back on his face.

"You're not going to win," he says, glancing between us. "There are too many of them, and their motives are too strong. The success of this technology is going to make a lot of people very rich. They aren't going to let you get in the way."

He almost looks apologetic.

Clearly, that's just my eyes playing tricks on me though, because he gives us one last look, turns around, steps into the portal, and disappears.

Chapter 15

As Dirk walks through the portal, I feel Kat start to shake.

It breaks my heart.

I wrap my other arm around her, and just stand there and hug her while she sobs.

"Kat, shhh..." I say gently. "It's okay, we'll figure it out, I promise we will."

But, I don't know how we'll figure it out, and I'm scared.

"Oh, Thomas," she says,"I'm not crying! I'm laughing! It worked!"

Wait, what?

She steps away from me and looks up at my face. She's not crying, not at all, she looks like she's just won an epic battle!

"He took it across, I totally tricked that little turd, and he walked it right out of the game for me!"

She dances around the room, making these tiny hops on her toes while she points her fingers in the air, like an absurd jitterbug.

"What," I ask. "what are you talking about?" How could he have taken it across? She never gave it to him. She never even mentioned it to him.

"My plan worked, Thomas," she laughs. "That's why I tackled him! I dropped the ring down the back of his shirt when I was pushing him to the ground! When he walked through the portal, he was taking the beacon out of the game, and he didn't even realize it!"

Wow! I'm amazed at the genius of this girl!

"That is awesome, way to go!"

I grab her and give her a big hug. Then I step back and look around.

Nothing looks the same, the game has completely changed in the span of a few seconds. The walls are cinder block, there's no furniture anywhere, and it all feels very....lame.

"Why does it look like this? What happened?"

"Oh, that," she says. "Yeah, I guess this is the first time you've witnessed it."

She spreads her arms, palms up. "Welcome to Soro's, the game as it really is."

"Wow." It's all I can say.

How did I spend so much time in this game? I went through interviews to work here! It was so important to me!

I feel angry, betrayed, and....used.

Like a pawn in someone else's game.

Which I was, literally.

"Well, I guess you were right."

It's a credit to her that she doesn't look TOO smug.

"So now what?" I look around, unsure of what happens next.

"Well, now you can decide if you want to keep playing. I mean a lot of people played before the beacon, so it was a good game, which is probably why The Company chose it to put one in it."

I guess that makes me feel a little better, but only a little bit.

"Is that why you got a job here and worked your way up to management, Kat? So you could locate the portal?"

"No," she says. "I could get to the portal whenever I wanted. I came here because I noticed such an increase in gameplay that I thought a beacon might be involved. I stayed because once I knew a beacon was here, I needed to find someone who could take it through."

That makes me think of something else I was going to ask her.

"Why didn't you just take it through yourself?"

"That's not what I do," she says. "I can't go through that portal any more than you can."

To prove it, she walks over to the swirling mist and sticks her hand through.

Nothing happens.

"So what do you do then?"

"That, my friend," she replies, "is a story for another day."

COME FIND TY ON YOUTUBE
@ TY THE HUNTER

Please leave a review,
they're so important.

The more reviews you leave,
the more books I write.

Ty

What Happens Next?

The World Keepers - Book 5

Other Books By Ty The Hunter

The Guild Crafters
Minecraft Themed Series
Ages 9 +

The Guild Crafers Block Books Series
Ages 4 +

Made in the USA
Middletown, DE
29 May 2022

66397059R00073